SCOOBY-DOO!

& THE
MUMMY
MYSTERY

SCOOBY-DOO & THE MUMMY MYSTERY

ISBN 1 84023 977 8

Published by Titan Books, a division of
Titan Publishing Group Ltd.
144 Southwark St
London SE1 0UP

SCRIPT: Dan Abnett, John Rozum, Frank Strom, Terrance Griep Jr.
PENCILS: Joe Staton, Anthony Williams
INKS: Dave Hunt, Jim Amash, Jeff Albrecht, Scott MacRae,
Andrew Pepoy, Dan Davis.
LETTERS: Tom Orzechowski, John Constanza,
Jared K. Fletcher, Jenna Garcia & Gustav.
COLOURS: Paul Becton, Sno Cone & Digital Chameleon

A CIP catalogue record for this title is available from
the British Library.

First edition: October 2004

10 9 8 7 6 5 4 3 2 1

Printed in Italy.

What did you think of this book? We love to hear from
our readers. Please email us at: readerfeedback@titanemail.com,
or write to us at the above address. You can also visit us at
www.titanbooks.com

DAN ABNETT writer
JOE STATON pencils
DAVE HUNT inks
JOHN COSTANZA letters
PAUL BECTON colors
HARVEY RICHARDS assists
HEIDI MacDONALD edits

THEY SAY THIS PYRAMID SET IS A *PERFECT* COPY OF PHARAOH PHUTT'S TOMB.

SAY, DIDN'T THE PHARAOHS BURY THEMSELVES WITH FOOD FOR THE AFTERLIFE?

mmmm

HA, SHAGGY, I DON'T THINK YOU'LL FIND ANY FOOD AROUND HERE.

NONE OF THIS IS REAL! LOOK, EVEN THE *WALLS* AREN'T *SOLID*!

WHOOAA!

FREDDIE!

SHLINK!

RUH, OH!

LIKE, *PUSH*, SCOOB! WE'VE GOT TO GET FREDDIE OUT OF THERE!

R'M ROOSHING, R'M ROOSHING!

SHLINK!

OOFFF!

ROOFFF!

F-FREDDIE?

THE LIBRARY LURKER

writer **JOHN ROZUM**
letterer **COSTANZA**
penciller **ANTHONY WILLIAMS**
colorist **PAUL BECTON**
assistant editor **HARVEY RICHARDS**
inker **JIM AMASH**
editor **HEIDI MacDONALD**

HEY! HOW COME YOU GET ALL THE LEFTOVER FOOD?

ROGGY RAGS!

BREAKFAST SPECIAL

I SURE WISH WE HAD TIME TO STICK AROUND AND SOLVE THIS MYSTERY!

FORGET IT, FRED. WE'RE ALREADY RUNNING LATE!

COOLSVILLE COURIER
BEASLEY JEWELS STOLEN
THIEVES STEAL BOOK SAFE FULL OF GEMS

HEY, WHAT'S THIS?

UH-OH, NOW VELMA'S AT IT!

"TREASURE ISLAND." IT'S A LIBRARY BOOK AND IT'S WAY OVERDUE!

TREASURE ISLAND
ROBERT LOUIS STEVENSON

THE LIBRARY'S RIGHT NEXT TO WHERE WE PARKED THE MYSTERY MACHINE. LET'S DROP IT OFF.

LIKE, AS LONG AS WE DON'T HAVE TO READ IT, THAT PIRATE, LONG JOHN SILVER, GIVES ME THE CREEPS.

:BRRR:

JEEPERS! THIS PLACE IS ENORMOUS.

AND DARK. LIKE, HOW CAN ANYBODY READ IN THIS DIM LIGHT?

WHERE IS EVERYBODY?

HELLO?

HELLO HELLO HELLO

REEPY.

LIKE, YOU SAID IT, SCOOB. LET'S RETURN THAT BOOK AND GET OUT OF HERE.

OKAY, THERE'S THE RETURN COUNTER.

I WONDER WHY NOBODY'S MANNING THE DESK?

BECAUSE I ORDERED THEM TO LEAVE!

LONG JOHN SILVER!

LIKE, I THOUGHT HE WAS ONLY MAKE-BELIEVE.

SO DID I!

LEAVE, LEST YOU WANTS TO BE SWINGING FROM A JIB-ARM INSTEAD.

THAT'S ALL WE NEEDED TO HEAR.

THERE ARE YOUR JEWEL THIEVES, MRS. BEASLEY.

THEY USED A COMBINATION OF COSTUMES AND SPECIAL EFFECTS TO SCARE PEOPLE AWAY FROM THE LIBRARY.

DR. JEKYLL CHANGED INTO MR. HYDE USING SPECIAL MAKEUP THAT ONLY SHOWED UP UNDER A BLACK LIGHT, JUST LIKE THE WITCH'S EVIL SPIRITS.

WE WERE ABLE TO SOLVE THE CASE BECAUSE LONG JOHN-- I MEAN TIM LEHNERT-- LEFT THE RECEIPT FROM THE COSTUME STORE IN THE COPY OF TREASURE ISLAND HE CHECKED OUT.

BUT WHO'S THE WITCH? SHE'S NOT ONE OF US.

TA-DA, IT'S JUST ME, DAPHNE.

THERE'S JUST ONE UNSOLVED PART TO THIS MYSTERY. WHERE ARE THE JEWELS?

I THINK I CAN SOLVE THAT, YOUNG MAN.

I'VE SOMETIMES FORGOTTEN WHERE I'VE SHELVED THIS BOOK ON MY OWN LIBRARY AT HOME, SO I HAD THIS LOCATOR INSTALLED IN THE BINDING.

WELL, I GUESS THAT WRAPS UP THIS CASE.

BEEP! BEEP BEEP-BEEP

YOU'RE OVERLOOKING ONE LITTLE PIECE OF UNSOLVED BUSINESS-- WHERE DID SHAGGY AND SCOOBY VANISH TO?

I THINK I KNOW THE ANSWER TO THAT!

...ROIL RAND RERVE!

SOUNDS MOUTHWATERING, SCOOB! HOW ABOUT THIS ONE-- POTATOES AU GRATIN WITH SAUTEED SPIN--

SHAGGY! SCOOBY!

Recipes

COOK BOOK

THERE YOU ARE! IT'S TIME TO GO. WE'RE ALREADY BEHIND SCHEDULE.

RHUT, RE'RE REST RETTING TO RUN ROOD RART!

NOW, SCOOBY. YOU TOO, SHAGGY.

OKAY, OKAY, WE GET THE PICTURE, DAPHNE.

SOMETIMES YOU CAN BE SUCH A WITCH.

The End

THE FRIGHT BEFORE CHRISTMAS!

FRANK STROM -- writer
JOE STATON -- penciller * DAVE HUNT -- inker
TOM ORZECHOWSKI -- letterer * PAUL BECTON -- colorist
DIGITAL CHAMELEON -- separations

'TWAS THE NIGHT BEFORE THE NIGHT BEFORE CHRISTMAS...

FIVE O'CLOCK AT LAST! HEADING *HOME*, BOB?

ME? ARE YOU KIDDING?

SCROOGE INC.
ACCOUNTING,
TAX PREPARATION
& LOANS

I'VE STILL GOT *CHRISTMAS SHOPPING* TO DO!

YOU'LL HAVE TO DO IT LATER, CRATCHET--I NEED YOU TO WORK *OVERTIME!*

...WHO WILL SHOW YOU THE ERROR OF YOUR WAYS! BE AFRAID!

I AM! I AM! BUT I KNOW WHAT TO DO ABOUT IT...

HELLO? MYSTERY INC.?

...AND THIS "GHOST" OF YOURS JUST APPEARED OUT OF THIN AIR?

THAT'S CORRECT, YOUNG MAN. I MUST SAY, I COULD HARDLY BELIEVE IT!

YOU AND ME BOTH. I DON'T BUY IT!

FRED! LOOK AT THESE MARKS ON THE FLOOR. THIS PROVES THE GHOST--OR SOMETHING-- WAS HERE LAST NIGHT!

SCROOGE, IN ACCOUNTING TAX PREPARATION & LOANS

WELL, HE COULDN'T HAVE COME IN THROUGH THE WINDOW-- IT'S LOCKED TIGHT.

MAYBE FROM THE CLOSET? HMM. PROBABLY NOT.

HE HAD TO COME FROM SOME- WHERE!

'TIS THE THOUGHT THAT COUNTS. BUT YOU WEREN'T THINKING THIS YEAR!

I...I...I WASN'T?

NO!!

LOOK YONDER-- IN THE WEE SMALL HOURS, A LIGHT BURNS IN THE CRATCHET HOUSE! THE FAMILY STILL WAITS AS CRATCHET SLAVES AWAY AT YOUR SHOP!

ALL TINY TIM WANTS FOR CHRISTMAS IS FOR HIS FATHER TO BE HOME WITH HIM!

WHAT KIND OF HEARTLESS JERK MAKES A GUY WORK AT CHRISTMAS TIME?

THAT JERK IS YOU, SCROOGE...!

OH, YEAH... I FORGOT. ∮SNIFF!∮ THAT POOR KID...

RREAH, RRROOR KID...

C'MON, SHAGGY! LET US OUT ALREADY! WE'RE MISSING EVERYTHING!

WHA--?

CREE-EE-EAK!

WELL, HERE'S ONE THING WE DIDN'T MISS-- A TRAP DOOR AND SECRET PASSAGE!

IN MY CLOSET? I HAD NO IDEA! BUT WHERE DOES IT LEAD?

STRAIGHT TO YOUR *SHOP,* OF COURSE!

CRATCHET

WHY, THIS IS *CRATCHET'S* CUBICLE! HE MUST BE THE *CULPRIT!*

A REASONABLE DEDUCTION. CHECK OUT THIS BOX OF "*OFFICE SUPPLIES*" HE'S STASHED UNDER HIS DESK!

SPOOK SUITS! VELMA, I THINK WE'VE FOUND OUR "*GHOST!*"

LIKE, CAN THESE GHOSTS GET ANY *CREEPIER?* I DUNNO ABOUT *YOU,* SCOOB, BUT I SURE DON'T WANNA FIND OUT!

LET'S GET THIS DOOR *OPEN* BEFORE...

EBENEEZER...!

Y-Y-YOIKS!!

I AM THE *GHOST OF CHRISTMAS FUTURE...!*

G-G-GLAD TO MEET YOU! *WE* ARE THE GHOSTS OF CHRISTMAS *PAST--*

--LIKE, AS IN "*PAST TENSE!*" RUN FOR IT, SCOOBY-DOO!!

R'IM RRRUNNING! R'IM RRRUNNING!

THE END

ICY RECEPTION

FRANK STROM -- writer
ANTHONY WILLIAMS -- penciler * JEFF ALBRECHT -- inker
TOM ORZECHOWSKI -- letterer * PAUL BECTON -- colorist
DIGITAL CHAMELEON -- separations

MS. ROTTENOVA-- YOU'RE NATASHA'S MAIN RIVAL. WHAT DO *YOU* KNOW ABOUT THESE GHOSTS?

DON'T *INSULT* ME. I CAN *BEAT* KRYLOVA WITHOUT RESORTING TO *TRICKERY!*

THIS IS A MOST *UNUSUAL* INVESTIGATION. WE ARE UNCERTAIN HOW TO PROCEED.

LEAVE IT TO *US*, OFFICER. MYSTERY OR NO MYSTERY, WE'VE GOT TO PROTECT NATASHA FROM ANY *DANGER!*

EXCUSE ME--DO YOU KNOW IF ANYONE'S BEEN WAY UP *THERE?*

ABOVE THE *BALCONY?* NYET. THAT AREA IS ONLY USED FOR *TV EQUIPMENT.*

HMM...

YOU ARE VERY *KIND*, BUT I CAN'T HELP BEING A LITTLE *WORRIED.*

DON'T BE. YOUR *SAFETY* IS OUR *TOP PRIORITY!*

HEY! WHAT ABOUT *MY* SAFETY?!?

OH, I DIDN'T *ALWAYS* HATE HER. SHE WAS SO *CUTE* AS A CHILD WITH HER LITTLE *APPLE CHEEKS*, AND SHE COULD *SPIN* LIKE A *TOP!* I THOUGHT SHE WAS *ADORABLE*...

...BUT THEN SHE STARTED *BEATING ME*, THE LITTLE *PEASANT!!* I COULD *KILL* HER!

ER...IS JUST *FIGURE* OF *SPEECH*, DOLLINK. YOU'RE NOT GOING TO *POLICE?*

NO, NO-- I JUST WANT A *LOOK* AT THE *TV EQUIPMENT.*

HMM, CAMERAS... MICROPHONES-- NOTHING OUT OF THE ORDINARY.

EXCEPT... ONE PIECE OF EQUIPMENT IS *MISSING!*

THAT'S IT!!

YOW! WATCH WHERE YOU'RE GOING, SHAGGY! WHAT GIVES?

G-G-GHOSTS! THE ICE IS FULL OF 'EM!!

CALM DOWN. THEY'RE GONE--VANISHED WITHOUT A TRACE.

OH, THEY LEFT A TRACE, ALL RIGHT. THESE IMPRESSIONS IN THE SNOW LOOK LIKE THEY WERE MADE BY A CAMERA TRIPOD...

...AND THAT PROVES MY THEORY!

THESE "GHOSTS" CAN'T HURT YOU, SHAGGY--THEY'RE PROJECTIONS.

WHOEVER IS BEHIND THIS IS USING STOLEN LIGHTING EQUIPMENT FROM THE ARENA TO PROJECT "GHOSTS" ONTO THE ICE!

WHEW! THAT'S GREAT, BUT WHO WOULD WANT TO SCARE NATASHA? FATHER FROST?

NOBODY'S ACTUALLY SEEN FATHER FROST. MARIA ROTTENOVA IS THE MOST LIKELY CULPRIT--SHE'S GOT THE MOTIVE, AND NOTHING TO LOSE!

WHY, THAT'S TERRIBLE!

NO--THAT'S TERRIFIC! NOW THAT I KNOW THE GHOSTS ARE FAKE, NOTHING CAN STOP ME FROM WINNING THE COMPETITION!

AND SO...

NO SIGN OF MARIA OR FATHER FROST ANYWHERE!

BAD LUCK FOR THEM--THEY'RE GONNA MISS NATASHA SKATING HER WAY TO A GOLD MEDAL!

THE END

"...WHILE SHAGGY, SCOOBY AND I WILL SEARCH THE *MOAT* FOR CLUES."

THIS CAR WE PARKED NEXT TO... I WONDER IF SOMEONE'S TRYING TO *DISGUISE* IT FOR A GETAWAY?

RAREN'T ROU ROGETTING RUMTHING, RELM...UH, REDDY?

FORGETTING SOMETHING? FORGETTING *WHAT?*

ROOBY RAX! ROR RAVERY!

RUB RUB
RUB RUB

SCOOBY SNAX FOR *BRAVERY?* BUT WHAT'S THERE TO BE AFRAID OF? IT'S ONLY A MONSTER.

NOW LET'S MAKE TRACKS. IT'S NOT LIKE THIS MOAT-THING IS GOING TO COME TO *US*...

!!!!!!!

UH OH...

WHAT'S THAT PHRASE VELMA ALWAYS USES...? "GENIES"? "JEEPLES"?

JINKIES!

HSSSSSS!

REAT RY REET, ROOB!

YIPE-YIPE-YIPE!

SCOOBY! SHAGGY! LEAD HIM THIS WAY!

HSSSSSS!

DIDN'T YOU TWO HEAR ME? I SAID...

UT!

FWUMP

OH, NO--MY... HER GLASSES!

SPLSSH

»WHIMPER«

SCOO...SHAGGY, LURE THE MOAT-THING AROUND THE MOAT ONCE, THEN BRING HIM ACROSS THE DRAWBRIDGE!

RURE RHE ROAT-RING-- RRRI-I-I-I-IGHT!

HSSSSSS!

UGH. SHE REALLY CAN'T SEE WITHOUT HER GLASSES.

SCOOBY, WATCH FOR THE MOAT-THING. I'LL TURN THE DRAWBRIDGE INTO A MONSTER TRAP... SOMEHOW!

BLOOP   BLOOP

"...THAT THE OTHERS ARE DOING BETTER THAN *WE* ARE!"

ACCORDING TO WHAT DR. ERROL SAID, WE SHOULD FIND A LEVER WHICH WILL OPEN A NEARBY SECRET PASSAGE...

WOW... I COULD LOOK ALL DAY. SEEING *WITHOUT GLASSES* IS...

BINK

YOWTCH--!

HEY--!

CAREFUL WITH *MY HEAD*, VELMA! DO YOU KNOW WHAT IT TAKES TO GET MY HAIR TO LOOK LIKE THIS?

SORRY, DAPHNE. I GUESS I'M NOT USED TO BEING *TALL*, EITHER.

KHRKHRKHRK

WHAT'S THAT NOISE? IT SOUNDS LIKE STONE CHAFING AGAINST STONE...

LOOK! WE FOUND THE SECRET PASSAGE!

SAY, ARE YOUR... UH, FRED'S SHOES *SQUEAKING...?*

OH. IT'S JUST BATS.

AIIIIEEEE!

WITNESS, CHILDREN, AS I *UNDO* THE MAD SCIENCE OF MY ARCHFOE!

ZAP

!

WH-WHAT...? IT WAS PROGRAMMED FOR ALL ARTIFICIAL LIFE FORMS!

THAT'S BECAUSE THE MOAT-THING *ISN'T* AN ARTIFICIAL LIFE FORM, DOCTOR...

YOU SEE? IT'S...

...*HUMAN?*

...OH!

YUGOR'S *HUMP!* THAT'S *YUGOR* IN THERE! *YOU* HAVE BEEN UNDERMINING MY EXPERIMENTS?

BUT *WHY*, LOYAL SERVANT... *WHY?*

"SERVANT"...*BAH!* I HAVE *ALWAYS* BEEN YOUR INTELLECTUAL SUPERIOR, "MASTER!" I SOUGHT TO SCARE YOU AWAY AND TAKE OVER YOUR LAB, RATHER THAN TOIL SECRETLY IN THIS *HIDEAWAY.*

AND I WOULD HAVE *GOTTEN AWAY* WITH IT, IF NOT FOR THESE *JUMBLED-UP KIDS!*

AUSTRALIA-- THE LAND DOWN UNDER!

A COUNTRY WITH UNUSUAL *WILDLIFE* AND AN EXTREMELY DELICATE *ECOSYSTEM* THAT MUST BE PROTECTED!

HERRIOT
WILDLIFE
PRESERVE

POACHING STRICTLY
PROHIBITED

QUIET *NIGHT*, EH, JED?

NOT ALL *THAT* QUIET, MATE! GOT SOME WONKY NOISES OVER IN *SECTOR-7.* CHECK IT OUT!

WONKY NOISES, HE SAYS! IT'S A *WILDLIFE RESERVE*-- IT'S *FILLED* WITH WONKY NOISES!

RUSSLE
RUSSLE

SCRAPE

HMM. THEN AGAIN, COULD BE *POACHERS!*

OI! YOU IN THE *BUSH!* LET'S HAVE A LOOK AT YOUR *SECURITY PASS,* EH?

OUR *SECURITY* IS EXTREMELY TIGHT. IT'S *DESIGNED* TO KEEP OUTSIDE ANIMALS AWAY!

SOUNDS LIKE YOU'RE *AFRAID* OF SOMETHING!

THAT'S RIGHT-- *HOUSE CATS.*

HOUSE CATS? ARE YOU *SERIOUS?*

COMPLETELY. CATS AREN'T *NATIVE* TO THIS COUNTRY. AT SOME POINT, THEY WERE BROUGHT IN ILLEGALLY AND HAVE BRED IN STAGGERING NUMBERS.

THESE CATS RUN WILD ALL OVER AUSTRALIA, HAVING REGRESSED TO A *FERAL* STATE. THEY'RE A MAJOR *THREAT* TO OUR NATIVE WILDLIFE, AND THAT'S THE VERY REASON WE'VE ESTABLISHED THIS RESERVE-- TO *PROTECT* AUSTRALIA'S ANIMALS!

GETTING BACK TO OUR MYSTERY... ARE THERE ANY *SUSPECTS?* ANY *BUSINESS RIVALS,* MAYBE?

I'M AFRAID NOT. WE'RE *GOVERNMENT- SANCTIONED* AND OWN THE LAND OUTRIGHT. WE BOUGHT THE PROPERTY *YEARS* AGO FROM *FARNHAM INDUSTRIAL.*

THAT'S GOTTA BE IT-- *FARNHAM'S* INVOLVED!

NO, I THINK IT HAS TO BE *POACHERS,* DAPHNE. THEY'RE THE ONLY PEOPLE WHO'D *PROFIT* FROM THIS SCAM!

GUYS? AREN'T YOU *FORGETTING* SOMETHING? WHAT IF THERE'S --GULP-- A *REAL* SABERTOOTH TIGER?

SHAGGY, AREN'T *YOU* FORGETTING SOMETHING? THE SABERTOOTH TIGER IS *EXTINCT!*

BAH! THERE IS NO *CONCLUSIVE PROOF* THE SABERTOOTH IS EXTINCT!

WHA--?!? WHO ARE *YOU?*

NORBERT BURKE, NATURALIST AND EXPERT TRACKER, AT YOUR SERVICE!

BELIEVE YOU ME, MATES, I'VE TRACKED DOWN MORE ELUSIVE BEASTIES THAN YOU CAN SHAKE A STICK AT! SO WHO'S GONNA *HELP* ME SNIFF OUT THIS SABERTOOTH, EH?

SORRY-- WE'VE GOT TO INVESTIGATE *FARNHAM INDUSTRIAL!*

AND I WANT THIS GUARD TO HELP ME CHECK THE *SECURITY SYSTEM!*

THAT'S THE SPIRIT! GOOD OF YOU TO *VOLUNTEER,* BOYS!

WHO... *US?!?*

RUH?

I FOUND THE TIGER HIDING IN THE BUSH, BUT ISN'T IT POSSIBLE HE'S HOLED UP IN ONE OF THOSE *CAVES?*

LET'S CHECK ON THE *SECURITY FENCES* FIRST.

I HAVE A HUNCH OUR *SABERTOOTH* WAS BROUGHT IN FROM *OUTSIDE.* WHEN I GET A *HUNCH,* I'M ALMOST *ALWAYS* RIGHT...

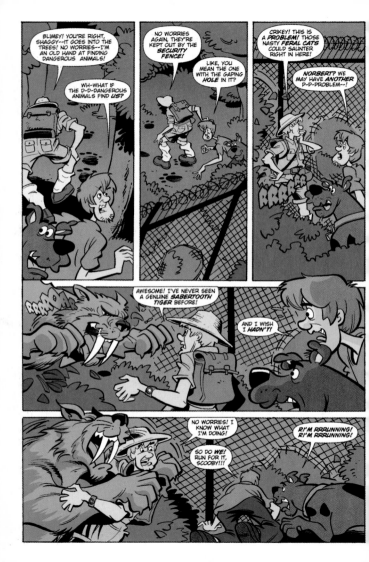

TEETH LIKE *KNIVES!* CLAWS LIKE *DAGGERS!* HE'S BIG AS LIFE!

A REAL SABERTOOTH? WELL, *THIS* PUTS AN UNEXPECTED TWIST ON THINGS!

DR. HERRIOT, DOES YOUR INSTITUTE HAVE ACCESS TO *FEDERAL ANIMAL REGISTRY* RECORDS?

EH? YES, OF COURSE.

FILE STORAGE
AUTHORIZED PERSONNEL ONLY

WE'RE CLOSELY ASSOCIATED WITH THE REGISTRY, AND SHARE INFORMATION WITH THEM.

ALL ON *COMPUTER,* OF COURSE. I'LL PUT IN MY ACCESS CODE AND YOU CAN HAVE A LOOK.

WHAT'S UP, VELMA?

JUST A *HUNCH,* DAPHNE.

VELMA, ISN'T THIS KIND OF A WASTE OF TIME? I MEAN, IF THE TIGER IS *REAL*--

THAT'S EXACTLY WHAT I'M LOOKING FOR-- A *REAL TIGER!*

GENTLEMEN, NOW THAT WE KNOW WHAT WE'RE DEALING WITH, WHAT SHOULD WE *DO?*

ONLY ONE THING *TO* DO, DOCTOR--

THAT'S JUST IT. I CHECKED THE *RECORDS* ON FARNHAM'S ZOO, AND HE HAPPENS TO OWN A TIGER THAT TURNS OUT TO BE OUR *SABERTOOTH*. FARNHAM PUT *FAKE FANGS* ON HIM!

BUT *WHY* WOULD HE PULL THIS CON ON HERRIOT?

THE ANSWER WAS IN ONE OF THE *CAVES*. SEE?

LOOKS LIKE... *ANCIENT FOSSILS?*

EXACTLY! PERFECTLY PRESERVED PREHISTORIC FOSSILS AND ARTIFACTS!

THEY'RE WORTH A HUGE *FORTUNE*, BUT FARNHAM NO LONGER OWNS THIS PROPERTY. HE PLANNED TO GET IT BACK BY *SCARING* HERRIOT, THEN SELLING THE LAND TO AN *ARCHAEOLOGICAL FOUNDATION!*

AND I WOULD'VE GOT AWAY WITH IT, TOO, IF NOT FOR YOU *MEDDLING KIDS*--!

THERE'S A GOOD TIGER! WE'LL RID THESE NASTY FANGS FOR YOU--!

PRETTY *SMART*, VELMA, BUT LET'S NOT FORGET *SHAGGY* AND *SCOOBY-DOO*-- THEY WERE AWFULLY *BRAVE* HANDLING THE TIGER!

AW, SHUCKS. THE *REAL* HEROES ARE THOSE LITTLE *CATS!*

YOU'RE RIGHT, SHAGGY! DON'T YOU THINK THEY DESERVE A *REWARD?*

SURE! BUT DO *WE* HAVE TO GIVE IT TO THEM--?

PURRRR....!

BRRR!

END

RUM DE DUM DE DUM...

!!

ROOPS!

WELL, SCOOBY, YOUR *WHISTLING* CERTAINLY HAS AN EFFECT ON PEOPLE!

WHAT'S GOING ON HERE?

SCOOBY WAS WHISTLING AND THIS ACTRESS JUST *FAINTED*.

EVERYONE KNOWS IT'S CONSIDERED *VERY UNLUCKY* TO WHISTLE BACKSTAGE!

THEY'RE NERVOUS *ENOUGH* ABOUT THE GHOST...AND YOUR FRIEND AND THE DOG AREN'T HELPING!

I'M SORRY, MR. LOVEY -- HONESTLY, SHAGGY AND SCOOBY *ARE* ONLY TRYING TO *HELP*...

I'M BEGINNING TO THINK THIS PLAY REALLY *IS* CURSED!

THE ACTORS ARE ALL JITTERY. AND THE POOR LEAD ACTOR IS *BESIDE HIMSELF.* HE DOESN'T KNOW IF HE CAN GO ON!

DON'T YOU WORRY, MR. LOVEY. I'VE GOT ONE LAST PLAN TO TRY.

JUST AS I THOUGHT. SHAGGY HEARD *FOOTSTEPS* WHEN HE WOKE UP AND SAW THE GHOST...

...BUT I DIDN'T HEAR THEM WHEN HE CAME UP BEHIND ME ON THE STAGE... AND THE *WHOLE GANG* SAW HIM THAT TIME.

SO THIS IS OUR *LAST CLUE...*

WHAT IS IT, SCOOBY?

ROOD!

BLOOD!

LIKE, YEUCH!

IT'S NOT *REAL* BLOOD, GUYS--IT'S THE *STAGE BLOOD* THE ACTORS USE.

LOOK, THERE'S MORE ON THE FLOOR!

IT LOOKS LIKE A *TRAIL...*

BUT WHO COULD IT BE?

LET'S FIND OUT!

IT'S AN *UNDERSTUDY*... BUT WHY?

AFTER FINDING THE NOTE AND THE DAGGER IN THE *STAR'S* DRESSING ROOM, I'D GUESS HE'S JEALOUS.

YOU MEAN HE WANTED TO PLAY *MACBETH* SO BADLY THAT HE TRIED TO *TERRIFY* MY STAR ACTOR?

AND HE NEARLY SCARED AWAY *ALL* MY ACTORS!

BUT HOW DID HE MOVE AROUND SO QUICKLY?

THAT'S THE *CLEVER* PART.

HE MADE A *FILM* OF HIMSELF IN COSTUME AND PROJECTED IT ONTO THE STAGE!

THAT'S WHY WE DIDN'T HEAR HIS *FOOTSTEPS* --AND WHY *YOU* DIDN'T NOTICE THE *COSTUME* WAS MISSING...

...UNTIL *SHAGGY* SAW THE REAL THING WHEN HE USED IT BETWEEN REHEARSALS!

I ONLY WANTED TO BE A STAR... JUST *ONCE*.

WELL, YOU'D BE A STAR IN THE *SPECIAL EFFECTS* DEPARTMENT, BUT NOT BEFORE YOU'VE PUT THIS MESS *RIGHT*!

LO, THE PERFORMANCE BEGINS...

LIKE, IT'S THE DUDE WITH THE DAGGER AGAIN!

REAH, RAGGY, RHIS IS RARY!

LIKE, DON'T WORRY, SCOOB. THEY DON'T NEED YOUR TONGUE, THEY'VE GOT ONE OF THEIR OWN!

RUH! RUKKY!

AND I'D LIKE TO THANK MY YOUNG FRIENDS HERE FOR MAKING THIS PRODUCTION OF MACBETH POSSIBLE!

LIKE, WHERE'S THE ACTOR IN THE SHAKESPEARE COSTUME?

WHAT? WE DON'T HAVE AN ACTOR PLAYING SHAKESPEARE.

YIKES!

LIKE, MAYBE SHAKESPEARE WANTED TO STOP THE JINX TOO?

ENCORE, SCOOBY! ENCORE!

HA! HA! HA!

HA!

THE END

TED! TED St. MORITZ! IT'S YOU!

I DIDN'T RECOGNIZE YOU IN THAT OUTFIT! I'LL BET YOUR OWN *MOTHER* WOULDN'T!

HEY, GUYS! HAVE YOU BEEN HERE LONG?

ACTUALLY, TED, WE JUST GOT HERE. WE HAVEN'T HAD A CHANCE TO LOOK AROUND.

WELL, THEN... LET ME SHOW YOU ON MY WAY TO THE TRACK!

SEE, EACH COMPETITOR--OR *SLIDER*--IN MY EVENT GETS TO MAKE FOUR RUNS FROM START TO FINISH, AND KEEPS HIS *BEST* TIME. SO FAR, I'M IN THE LEAD...

...KNOCK ON WOOD!

THIS PROPERTY IS SO *BEAUTIFUL*, TED... AND WHAT A *BIG* CROWD!

YEAH. THE ONLY PEOPLE NOT WATCHING THE *SKELETON CHAMPIONSHIP* ARE THE OCCUPANTS OF THE LOCAL *PRISON!*

"S-SK-SKELETON"?

OH, "SKELETON" JUST REFERS TO THE CHASSIS OF THE ORIGINAL SLEDS, WHICH RESEMBLED A SET OF *BONES.*

RONES...?

TRISTON SMITH!

RIGHT ON! TRISTON ASSUMED THE ROLE OF GHOST, KNOWING HE'D SCARE EACH SLIDER INTO CRASHING. THAT WAY, NO ONE WOULD NOTICE THAT THE JUDGE WAS MISSING. THEN...

WAIT A MINUTE, WAIT A MINUTE...

THIS DOESN'T MAKE ANY SENSE! BY HAUNTING THE TRACK, TRISTON SMITH WOULD ONLY RUIN HIS OWN RACE!

MAYBE, BUT HE'D MORE THAN MAKE UP THE DIFFERENCE BY *SMUGGLING INMATES* OUT OF THE LOCAL PRISON!

WHAAT? H-HOW...?

WHEN WE FIRST ARRIVED, WE DIDN'T RECOGNIZE TED BECAUSE OF HIS *OUTFIT*. THAT TURNED OUT TO BE OUR *FIRST* CLUE... EVEN BEFORE WE REALIZED WE'D STUMBLED UPON A MYSTERY!

THROUGH A HIDDEN TUNNEL LEFT OVER FROM THE OLD TOUCHWOOD LUMBER CAMP, MR. SMITH WAS ABLE TO SNEAK INMATES FROM THE PRISON AND INTO THE FINISH STATION.

WELL, SO WHAT--? THE SECOND A PRISONER LEFT THE STATION, HE'D JUST BE *RECAPTURED!*

NOT IF HE WAS *DISGUISED!* EACH INMATE WOULD EMERGE FROM THE FINISH STATION DRESSED AS A *SLIDER!*

A SLIDER? BUT...

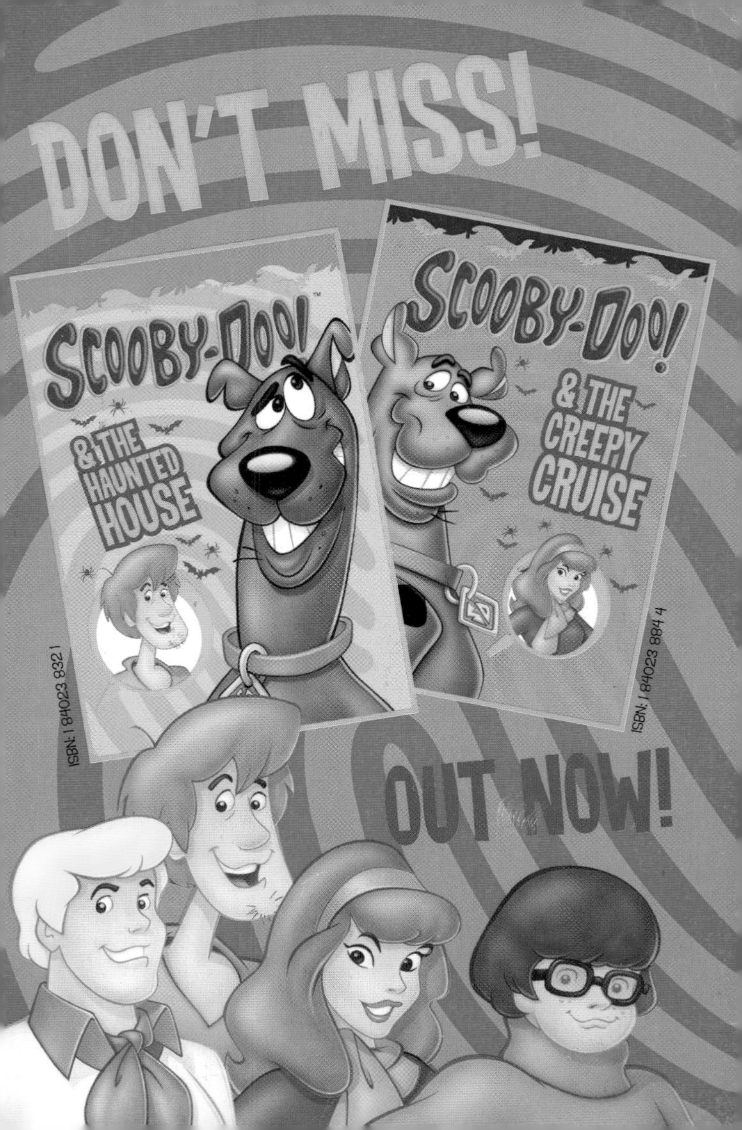

DON'T MISS!
SCOOBY-DOO!
& THE HAUNTED HOUSE
ISBN: 1 84023 832 1
SCOOBY-DOO!
& THE CREEPY CRUISE
ISBN: 1 84023 884 4
OUT NOW!